# Kate's Tricky Treat

Written by
**Slade Stone**

Illustrated by
**Danny Brooks Dalby**
**Leigh Anna Thompson**

All art and text ©Dalmatian Press.
ISBN: 1-57759-832-6
First published in the U.S. in 2002 by Dalmatian Press, LLC, U.S.A.

**Dalmatian Press**

02  03  04  NGS  5  4  3  2  1

Kate sat on her front step with her chin in her hand. "Halloween night," Kate sighed, "and Wilson had to go and break his leg."

"Hey, Kate—what's up?"

Kate looked up and saw two of the "cool" kids of Booville—Rattler Jones and Spike Meaney.

"Oh, hi, guys," Kate said. "I'm just sitting here waiting for my friends to go trick-or-treating. And I'm trying to think of a nice thing to do for Wilson—you know, he broke his leg today."

"Well aren't you a nice one," said Rattler. "Isn't she nice, Spike?"

"She's nice, Rattler. They don't get any nicer or sweeter than Kate. In fact... she's so nice, she's cool. I think *she* should come along with us tonight."

"Oh, golly," said Kate, "I can't. My friends will be here any minute."

"Hey, we don't invite many kids to hang out with us," said Spike. "Only the cool kids. It's a real treat to go out with Rattler and Spike. But if you don't want to be *cool*..."

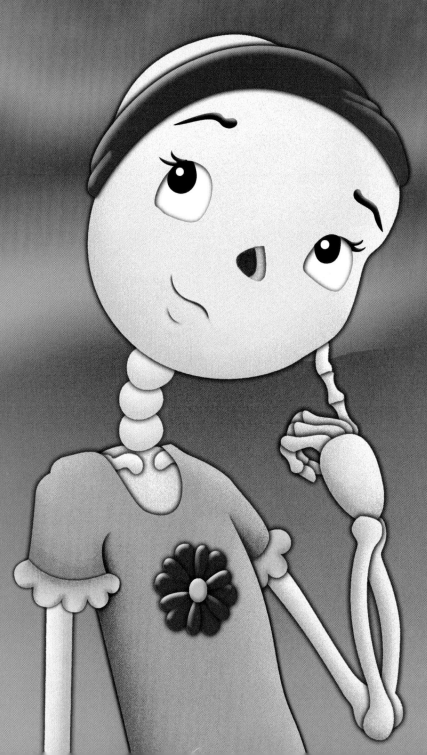

"Oh, I want to be cool!" stammered Kate. *I do want to be cool, don't I?* she thought to herself.

"Well, we're going," said Rattler. "And I think your friends have forgotten you, so come on! We're gonna scare up a bunch of fun!"

"Maybe my friends *did* forget me...," started Kate.

"Forget about them," interrupted Spike. "Let's rock and roll this town tonight!"
"Yeah! Let's rock and roll!" chimed in Kate. "I'll go change!"
*Wow! Out with the cool kids!* she thought.

At Mrs. Gizzard's house, Rattler, Spike and Kate were treated with bags of Gruesome Gumdrops. As they went down the sidewalk, Spike turned and smiled creepily at Kate.

"Now for the trick!" he snickered.

From out of his candy sack he pulled a carton of eggs.

"What are the eggs for?" asked Kate.

"For rockin' this town!" cried Spike. He picked out an egg and threw it at Mrs. Gizzard's new mailbox—*Crack!*—where it splattered!

"Ha-ha! That's great, Spike! Let me have one!" Rattler slung one onto the garden fence—*Splat.*

"Rattler! Spike!" cried Kate. "Why are you doing this?"

"Cool it, chickie-babe," said Rattler. "This is how we have fun on Halloween night. All the cool kids do it. The grown-ups expect this."

"They do?" asked Kate.

"Well, sure! Where ya been hiding? In a nicey-nicey cage?"

Rattler and Spike burst out laughing.

"Hey! Hey, I know how to have fun, too," said Kate.

Slowly, she picked up an egg and threw it at the birdbath.

It missed and broke on the ground.

It did *not* feel fun... or cool.

"Hey, come on! Some kids are coming! Let's scram!" said Spike.

Kate saw her friends, Frank Junior, Francine, and Denton, going up Mrs. Gizzard's walk. *I hope they didn't see me,* she thought.

At Mr. Creepout's house, they were treated with Booberry Jellybeans.

*Please don't throw more eggs,* thought Kate as they walked away.

In the shadows under a tree, Rattler pulled a big roll of toilet paper from his sack. "Now it's time to roll!" he giggled. He threw the roll over a big limb of a tree.

"Your turn!" Rattler said to Kate. "Now throw it hard—over that branch up there—and don't miss!"

"I don't know about this," said Kate nervously. "Why are we doing this to Mr. Creepout's tree?"

"Because it's Halloween, Miss Nicey-nicey. I told you we'd have fun—now toss it, or we'll leave you here and find someone else who wants to have fun."

Kate heaved a sigh, and then heaved the roll up over the branch. *What a shame to be messing up such a nice, scary tree,* she thought. *But I do want to impress my new friends.*

"All right!" said Rattler. "Now it's time for some real fun—Come on!"

They raced over to old Mr. Screech's house. Kate started down the walk—but Rattler and Spike stayed back.

"Aren't you getting a treat?" asked Kate.

"That's OK," whispered Rattler. "You just go on. Go up and ring the doorbell. And when old man Screech answers the door—we'll rock away at him!"

He held up more eggs.

"Oh, you wouldn't!" said Kate.

"Hey, Miss Goody-goody. Why do you think we wanted you along?" whispered Spike. "No one would *ever* suspect Kate of doing something tricky! If old man Screech saw us, he wouldn't open the door. Not after—hee-hee-hee—"

"Yeah! Hee-hee. Not after what we did to him *last* Halloween," giggled Rattler.

Kate glared at Rattler and Spike. "Oh, really? Well, let me tell you something! The reason no one would ever expect Kate to do something mean or tricky is because *Kate wouldn't!* I'm not going to help you—so there!"

She stamped her foot, then rushed at them with all her might and yelled,

"BOO!"

Rattler and Spike were so startled they dropped their bags. Rolls of paper tumbled out. The eggs went *Splat!* all over the sidewalk. Kate watched as the two "cool" kids ran off crying. Then she looked at the sidewalk.

"And Kate would never leave a mess like this, either," she said to herself.

Kate picked up the roll of paper and started to clean up the gooey mess.

Suddenly, she heard footsteps and looked over to see familiar shoes.

"Frank Junior!" she cried. "And Francine! Denton, is that you?"

"We went to your house, but you weren't there," explained Frank Junior.

"I know. I'm sorry. I left with Rattler and Spike—and I found out they're no friends of mine. Now I have a big mess to clean up."

"No, *we* have a mess to clean up," said Francine. "Come on, guys, let's help Kate."

For the next hour, the four friends cleaned up every egg and pulled down all the paper from Mr. Creepout's tree.

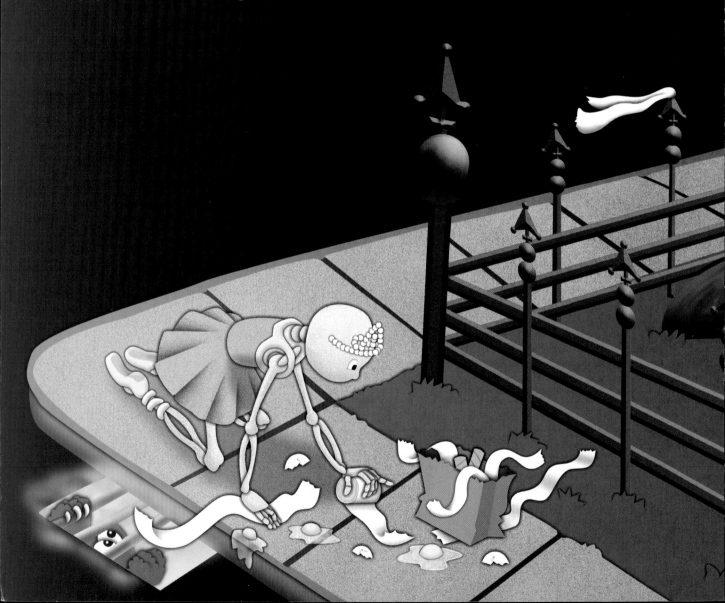

"I'm so lucky to have friends like you," said Kate softly. "Thank you. All of you."

"Sure thing, Kate," said Frank Junior. "We are always delighted to provide a friend with timely assistance. And I guess that just about wraps that up."

"Hey! Speaking of wrapping things up...," called out Denton. "Come on! We gotta get to Wilson's house and share our candy with him! Let's go!"

"Wow! Thanks, everybody!" said Wilson to all his friends who had come to spend the rest of Halloween night with him. "You guys are the coolest kids in Booville!"

Yes, *they are,* thought Kate.
*The coolest.*